Buddy's

Adapted by Andrea Posner-Sanchez
from the episode "T. Rex Teeth"

Based on the television series created by Craig Bartlett

Illustrated by Dave Aikins

A GOLDEN BOOK • NEW YORK

randomhouse.com/kids

pbskids.org/dinosaurtrain

ISBN: 978-0-375-86156-7

Printed in the United States of America

10 9 8 7 6 5 4 3 2 1

THE JIM HENSON COMPANY

www.henson.com

One day, Shiny was teaching her siblings how to play Dinosaur Hopscotch. "You stand here and toss your stick onto a square. Then hop to the end," she instructed.

Tiny and Don each had a turn.

"Buddy's next," said Shiny. "Buddy?"

But Buddy wasn't paying attention. He was chewing on his hopscotch stick.

Buddy bit down hard on the stick.
"Huh? My tooth came out!" he yelled. "One minute
it was in my mouth—and now it's out!"

Everyone rushed over to see.

"Why did my tooth fall out?" Buddy asked.

"You smile too much, and your teeth are tired out," Shiny suggested.

"That doesn't sound right," said Tiny.

Buddy ran to ask his mother.
Since Pteranodons don't have
teeth, Mrs. Pteranodon didn't
know much about them.

"Let's visit our friend Delores
Tyrannosaurus and ask her,"
she said.

Buddy liked that idea.
"Yeah, she's a T. rex,
just like me!"

Soon Buddy, Tiny, and Mrs. Pteranodon were on the Dinosaur Train. Mr. Conductor noticed something different about Buddy right away.

"Wasn't there one more tooth in your mouth the last time I saw you?" he asked.

"You're right, Mr. Conductor," Buddy replied.

Then Buddy showed
Mr. Conductor how he had
chewed on a stick and it
wiggled a tooth and . . .

. . . another tooth came out!
"Ack!" cried Buddy. "Are all
my teeth going to come out?"

"I don't know," Mr. Conductor told him, "but I see you're going to Rexville Station. The Tyrannosaurus there will know what's going on with your teeth."

The train soon pulled into the station, and Buddy led the way to the Tyrannosaurus nest. Delores and her daughter, Annie, were happy to see their friends.

"So, Buddy, are you having fun being a T. rex?" Annie asked.

"I love being a T. rex!" Buddy told her. "But today I've got a problem. I started losing my teeth!"

Delores told Buddy not to worry. "All T. rexes lose their teeth," she explained. "And then we grow new ones in place of the old ones."

Everyone peeked inside Buddy's mouth.
"Cool! Buddy, it's true," cried Tiny. "You've already got
new teeth coming in!"

Buddy was so happy, he did a little dance.
But then he had more questions. "Why does this
happen? And how often?"

"Our teeth are replaced all the time," Delores explained. "New ones come in as old ones get worn out."

"And our teeth get worn out because we're always chewing tough meat and bones," added Annie.

That reminded Delores that she hadn't offered her guests any lunch. "Are you hungry? We're having carrion," she said.

Tiny whispered to her mother, "Carrion is meat. Do we have to eat it?"

Mrs. Pteranodon said that she and Tiny weren't hungry and that they preferred fish, anyway. They watched as the T. rexes ate happily—and noisily!

"What do you have to do to keep your teeth clean?"
Tiny asked.

"Not a thing. The old ones fall out and new ones
grow in—it's wonderful!" Delores said with a laugh.

Delores continued eating and Tiny pulled her brother aside. "Whew! Her breath smells awful," she whispered.

"Did my breath smell bad before I ate the carrion?" Buddy asked.

"Uh, no," Tiny answered.

Then Buddy breathed on his sister. "How does it smell now?"

Tiny's expression proved what Buddy had thought: the bad breath was caused by what the T. rexes ate.

After lunch, everyone walked back to the train station. On the way, Buddy found a grown-up T. rex tooth.

"It's huge!" exclaimed Tiny. "And it has a sharp ridge on the side."

Buddy and Tiny took turns holding the big tooth up to their mouths.

As Buddy, Tiny, and Mrs. Pteranodon boarded the Dinosaur Train, they waved goodbye to Annie and Delores.

"Thanks for telling me about my teeth," Buddy said. "I feel so much better now!"

Back at home, everyone was getting ready to play Dinosaur Hopscotch again. This time, Buddy chewed on a leaf.

"Why are you eating a plant?" Tiny asked. "You're a carnivore, silly!"

"Mom said it's a leaf called mint. It's supposed to make your breath smell better," Buddy said.

Just then, Buddy remembered the grown-up T. rex tooth he had found. He showed it to Don and Shiny.

"Wow! Now, *that* is a tooth!" Shiny exclaimed. "I can't believe Buddy's going to be a giant T. rex someday."

"Yeah!" cried Buddy. "I'm going to have a mouthful of giant T. rex teeth like this one! RAARRR!"

"But you'll be nice—and you'll have minty-fresh breath!" Don said.